해피 투게더

〈K-픽션〉 시리즈는 한국문학의 젊은 상상력입니다. 최근 발표된 가장 우수하고 흥미로운 작품을 엄선하여 출간하는 〈K-픽션〉은 한국문학의 생생한 현장을 국내외 독자들과 실시간으로 공유하고자 기획되었습니다. 〈바이링궐 에디션 한국 대표 소설〉 시리즈를 통해 검증된 탁월한 번역진이 참여하여 원작의 재미와 품격을 최대한 살린 〈K-픽션〉 시리즈는 매 계절마다 새로운 작품을 선보입니다.

The K-Fiction Series represents the brightest of young imaginative voices in contemporary Korean fiction. This series spans a wide range of outstanding short stories selected by the editorial board of *ASIA* each season. These stories are then translated by professional Korean literature translators, all of whom take special care to convey the writers' original tones and nuances. We hope that these exceptional young Korean voices will delight all readers both here and abroad.

해피 투게더
Happy Together

서장원｜페이지 모리스 옮김
Written by Seo Jang-won
Translated from Korean by Paige Aniyah Morris

ASIA
PUBLISHERS

차례
Contents

해피 투게더
Happy Together

밖으로 나가기 직전, 나는 건물 층계참에 서서 창밖의 해주를 바라보았다. 해주는 구형 소나타에 기대서 있었다. 품이 넉넉한 검은 티셔츠에 면바지 차림이었고, 여름마다 고수하던 스타일대로 숱 많은 머리카락을 정수리 위로 틀어 올리고 있었다. 나는 심호흡을 하고 계단을 내려갔다. 곧 해주가 나를 발견하곤 손을 흔들어줬다. 걱정했던 것처럼 놀라거나 당황한 모습은 아니었다. 해주는 웃고 있었다. 마스크를 쓰고 있었지만 나는 그걸 알 수 있었다.

"뭐야. 너무 예뻐져서 못 알아보겠다."

Right before I went outside, I stood on the landing and watched Haejoo through the window. She was leaning up against an old Sonata. In a black, wide-cut T-shirt and jeans, she had her thick hair tied up into a bun atop her head, the same style she wore it in every summer. I took a deep breath, then went down the stairs. Right away, Haejoo spotted me and waved. She didn't seem surprised or flustered like I'd worried she would be. She was smiling. She had on a mask, but I could tell.

"What the hell? You got so pretty, I didn't recognize you," Haejoo said as soon as she saw me, her voice cheery and bright.

해주는 나를 보자마자 높고 경쾌한 톤으로 말했다.

"얼굴 보이지도 않는데, 오버하지 마."

나는 그렇게 말하며 마스크를 내려 해주가 보지도 않고 예쁘다고 칭찬한 얼굴을 내비쳤다.

"오버 아니야."

"넌 똑같은 거 같아."

"똑같긴, 늙었지. 눈 밑에 주름 봐."

"그건 그렇다. 나도 그래."

해주는 킬킬대면서 내가 들고 있던 커다란 가방을 받아 들었다. 가방 속에는 실내복 몇 벌과 약봉지들, 그리고 책한 권이 들어 있었는데, 내가 해주네에 머무는 동안 필요한 물건들이었다. 나는 일주일쯤 해주네 아파트에서 지내며 해주를 돌봐주기로 했다. 해주가 가방을 자동차 뒷좌석에 올려놓았다. 우리는 차에 탔다. 나는 한동안 조용히 있다가 자동차가 해방촌의 복잡한 골목길을 지나 넓은 도로로 빠져나왔을 때 해주에게 다시 말을 걸었다.

"어떻게 된 거야?"

해주는 어젯밤 내게 전화를 걸어 지난 한 달 동안의 일을 털어놓았는데, 상황이 좋지 않은 것 같았다.

"어제 얘기한 대로야. 그만 사는 거지 뭐."

"You can't even see my face, so quit exaggerating," I said, lowering my mask to reveal a glimpse of the face she had complimented before even seeing it.

"I'm not, I swear."

"Well, you look exactly the same."

"Come on, you know I've gotten old. Look at the wrinkles under my eyes."

"Oh, whatever. I've got them, too."

With a cackle, Haejoo took the big bag I was carrying. Inside were several sets of nightclothes and medicine packets, plus a book—all things I would need while I was staying at her place. I was spending the week looking after Haejoo at her apartment. She put my bag down on the backseat. We got in the car. For a while, I was quiet, but after we'd emerged from the complex side streets of Haebangchon and onto the main road, I started up the conversation again.

"So what happened?"

The night before, Haejoo had called and laid out the events of the past month. The situation didn't look too good.

"It's like what I told you yesterday. He's moving out."

"So you made up your mind?"

"Yep. We're getting divorced." She said this like it was nothing, tap, tap, tapping her forefinger on the

"마음 굳혔어?"

"응. 이혼할 거야."

해주는 검지로 핸들을 톡톡 두드리며 별일 아니라는 듯 말했다. 해주는 오래 전에 대학 동문인 민형과 결혼했는데, 두 사람이 결혼했을 무렵에 나는 해주와 민형 모두와 친구였다.

*

해주네 아파트에는 민형의 흔적이 그대로 남아 있었다. 결혼사진이 거실 벽에 걸려 있었고, 식탁에는 두 사람이 이것저것 일정을 적어놓은 달력이 세워져 있었다. 베란다에 놓인 건조대에는 민형의 와이셔츠며 실내복 여러 벌이 걸려 있었는데 해주는 집에 들어가자마자 그것들을 건조대에서 거두기 시작했다. 그러면서 내게는 예전처럼 작은 방을 사용하면 된다고 말해주었다. 나는 작은 방에서 옷을 갈아입고, 간단히 짐을 정리했다. 다시 거실로 나왔을 때에는 해주가 소파에 앉아 민형의 옷을 개고 있었다.

"다음에 오면 들려 보내려고."

wheel. A long time ago, Haejoo had married Minhyung, our college classmate. Around the time they got married, the three of us had been friends.

*

Traces of Minhyung had been left untouched around Haejoo's apartment. Wedding photos were hung up on the living room walls, and a calendar with the two of their various, scribbled-in dates sat propped up on the table. Minhyung's dress shirts and several of his nightclothes were hanging on the drying rack out on the balcony, and as soon as Haejoo stepped inside the house, she went and started pulling them all down. As she did, she told me I could take the smaller bedroom like I had before. I got changed in there and quickly unpacked my things. When I went back out into the living room, Haejoo was sitting on the sofa, folding Minhyung's clothes.

"So I can send them off with him the next time he comes by," she said.

It seemed a little like she was making excuses, picking up a T-shirt from the laundry heap and gently folding it once over the length, then the width. Minhyung had left home after the two of them got

해주는 다소 변명하는 것 같은 말투로 그렇게 말하고는, 빨래더미에 티셔츠를 집어 세로로 한 번, 가로로 한 번 단정히 접었다. 민형은 해주와 다툰 이후 집을 나가 며칠째 연락이 닿지 않는다고 했다. 해주는 아마 시댁에 가 있을 거라고 추측했지만 자세히는 모르는 것 같았고, 일부러 신경 쓰지 않으려 하는 눈치였다. 나는 소파에 앉아서 해주와 함께 민형의 옷을 개기 시작했다. 쌓여 있던 빨래더미를 거의 다 갰을 즘 해주는 이제 뭘 할까, 하고 한가로이 물었다. 그러고는 내가 뭐라 대답하기 전에 마트에서 재료를 사와 봉골레 파스타를 만들어 먹자고 제안했다. 모시조개를 화이트와인에 볶아 요리한 적이 있는데, 맛이 제법 그럴듯했다고 말이다. 나는 선뜻 그러자고 했다가 해주가 와인을 먹어선 안 되겠다는 생각이 들어 반대했다. 해주는 내일 오후에 임신중절수술을 앞두고 있었다.

*

한때 해주와 민형은 아이를 갖기 위해 노력했다. 결혼한 이듬해부터 일 년 남짓한 시간이었다고 기억한다. 결

into an argument, and it had been several days now since Haejoo last heard from him. She said she would guess that he'd gone to his parents' house, though she couldn't be sure, and I got the sense that she was deliberately pretending not to care. I took a seat on the sofa and began to fold Minhyung's clothes with her. We had almost finished folding all the clothes in the pile when Haejoo wondered aloud, "What should we do now?" Before I could answer, she suggested we go to the mart to pick up the ingredients for pasta alle vongole. She'd made the dish before, stir-frying the short-necked clams in white wine, and it had turned out surprisingly decent. I said sure, that was fine with me, but took it back when I remembered Haejoo shouldn't be having wine. She had an abortion scheduled for tomorrow afternoon.

*

There was a time when Haejoo and Minhyung had been trying for a baby. I remember that period lasting a little more than a year after they got married. It hadn't worked out in the end. After several attempts at IVF treatments failed, they gave up completely on the idea of having a child. Haejoo later told me she

과적으론 잘 되지 않았다. 몇 번 시도했던 시험관 시술이 모두 실패하고 나서, 두 사람은 아이를 갖는 것을 완전히 체념했다. 더 이상 배란주기에 일상의 리듬을 맞추고 싶지 않았다고, 나중에 해주가 내게 말해주었다. 그러고는 한동안은 두 사람 모두 술에 취해 지냈다. 나를 불러 딩크족 부부의 탄생을 축하하는 단출한 파티를 열기도 했는데, 그 파티는 곧 한 달에 한 번꼴로 열리는 정기적인 모임이 됐다. 주로 해주 부부가 날을 정해 나를 불렀고, 나는 와인을 사들고 해주네 아파트로 갔다. 그러고는 밤늦게까지, 때로는 동이 틀 무렵까지 술을 마셨다. 그러다 너무 취기가 오르면 베란다로 나가 문을 열어놓고 밤바람을 쐈다. 나는 지금도 거기서 두 친구와 함께 서 있던 밤들을 기억한다. 언젠가는 듬성듬성 불 켜진 건너편 아파트를 바라보면서, 민형이 저기로 이사를 오라고 내게 농담을 한 적도 있다. 그러면 매일 셋이서 술을 마실 수 있다고 말이다. 내 월급으로는 어림없는 소리였다. 그 시절에 나는 작은 출판사에 다니며 박봉을 받고 있었다. 어쩌다 늦은 밤 사무실에 혼자 남게 되면, 나는 탁상 달력을 뒤적거리며 해주 부부가 언제 또 나를 불러줄지 셈해보곤 했다. 어쩌면 나는 두 사람이 내가 없는 시간에도 그렇

hadn't wanted to match the rhythm of her daily life to her ovulation cycles anymore. So for a while, the two of them spent all their time getting drunk. They called to tell me they were holding a small party to celebrate the birth of themselves as a DINK couple, but it soon ended up being a regular gathering that took place once a month. Most times, they would set the date and call me up, and I'd go out and buy some wine to bring over to Haejoo's apartment. Then we'd stay up drinking until late at night, sometimes into the early hours of the morning. When we got too tipsy, we would slide open the door to the balcony and go out to get some fresh air. Even now, I remember the nights I spent there with the two of them, my friends. Once, as we were looking out at the apartment building across the street with a smattering of windows lit up here and there, Minhyung joked that I should move in there. Then the three of us could drink together every night. I said it wouldn't work out given my salary. At the time, I was working at a small publisher for next to nothing. When I found myself alone in the office late at night, I would check my desk calendar and count how long until Haejoo and Minhyung called me over again. Somehow, I must have vaguely believed the two of them kept up that same festive mood even when I

듯 즐거운 분위기를 유지할 거라고 막연하게 믿었던 것 같다.

그러나 며칠 전에 민형은 자신은 아이 없는 삶에 만족한 적이 없다고 폭언을 했다. 며칠 내내 이어진 해주와의 다툼 끝에 나온 말이었다. 당장 아이를 낳는 일이며 아이를 키우는 데 드는 품과 돈과 시간을 도저히 감당할 수 없다는 해주와 달리, 민형은 오래 기다린 아이를 반드시 낳아야 한다고 주장했다. 해주가 아이를 가졌단 소식을 듣자마자 민형이 가장 먼저 한 말은 '오래 기다린 축복'이었다.

"축복이라니 기막히지?"

해주는 칼국수 면을 우물거리면서 말했다. 우리는 부엌의 둥근 식탁에 마주 앉아 있었다. 아직 바깥에는 저녁빛이 남아 있었지만 식탁 위의 노란 전등을 켜놓았고, 그 불빛이 해주의 머리 위에 금빛 테두리를 만들었다.

"그러게 축복이라니."

나는 옛 친구의 실언에 고개를 절레절레 흔들었다.

"그래도 좋다."

해주가 또 말했다.

"좋다니 뭐가?"

wasn't around.

But a few days ago, Minhyung had lashed out at Haejoo about how he'd never been happy being childless. For the next few days, he ended every argument they had with those words. Unlike Haejoo, who said she couldn't handle all the labor, money, and time she would need to have and raise a child, Minhyung insisted they needed to go ahead and have the baby they'd been waiting such a long time for. As soon as he found out she was pregnant, the first thing Minhyung said was that it was "a long-awaited blessing."

"A blessing, can you believe that?" Haejoo said, chewing her kalguksu noodles. We sat across from each other on either side of the round kitchen table. The evening light was still shining outside, but the light above the table was on, too, and cast a gold outline around Haejoo's head.

"A blessing. Yeah, right." I shook my head at how my old friend had put his foot in his mouth.

"Still, this is nice," she said.

"What is?"

"I feel like it's gotten easier to talk with you about this stuff. Of course, it was easy before, too. But still."

"Yeah. That part is nice."

"너랑 이런 얘길 하는 게 더 편해진 느낌이야. 물론 전에도 그랬지만."

"그래, 그건 참 좋네."

우리는 막 한패가 된 악당들처럼 낄낄댔다. 잠시 뒤 웃음을 멈춘 해주가 내 어깨 너머로 어둑한 거실을 바라봤다.

"사실 그전부터 많이 변했어. 요즘엔 집에 오면 맨날 저기 누워서 유튜브만 봤거든."

나는 고개를 돌려 해주가 '저기'라고 말한, 가죽이 반들반들 닳은 소파를 바라보았다. 민형이 누웠던 자리에는 해주와 내가 개켜놓은 민형의 옷들이 가지런히 쌓여 있었다.

"사실은 그게 정말 싫었어."

"퇴근하고 누워 있는 거?"

"아니, 유튜브 보는 거. 영화 해설하는 이상한 채널을 보거든. 멍청한 소리 늘어놓는 유튜버들 있잖아. 그리고 얼마 전에는,"

해주는 거기까지 말하고 호흡을 한번 가다듬었다.

"왕가위 보고 '재능충'이라고 했어. 그게 뭐 재미난 말인 것처럼."

나는 재능충이란 말을 곱씹으며 고개를 끄덕였다. 나

We snickered like a pair of villains. A moment later, Haejoo stopped laughing and looked over my shoulder into the dim living room.

"Honestly, he's changed a lot. Lately, whenever he got home, he'd just lie down over there and watch YouTube."

I turned my head to look at the "over there" Haejoo was referring to—a sofa with its leather worn smooth. She and I had neatly piled his clothes on the spot where he'd lie down.

"To tell you the truth, I really hate it."

"What? Him coming home from work and lying down?"

"No, him watching YouTube. He watches those weird movie commentary channels. With those YouTubers who just run off at the mouth about whatever nonsense, you know. And not too long ago"—Haejoo paused to clear her throat—"he said Wong Kar-wai was 'a fuckin' wizard.' Like that was such a funny thing to say."

I nodded, mulling over that phrase: "a fuckin' wizard." Haejoo, Minhyung, and I had all met for the first time in a college film club. It was the year Wong Kar-wai's *In the Mood for Love* came out, and we were all his fans.

와 해주, 그리고 민형은 대학교 영화 동아리에서 처음 만났다. 왕가위 감독의 〈화양연화〉가 개봉하던 해였고, 우리는 모두 왕가위의 팬이었다.

*

다음 날 나와 해주는 택시를 타고 병원으로 갔다. 해주는 담담했다. 택시 안에서도, 병원 복도를 오가며 이런저런 검사를 받는 동안에도 특별히 긴장한 것 같지는 않았다. 회복실에서 수액을 맞으며 수술을 기다릴 때, 내가 무섭지 않느냐고 묻자 해주는 별로, 하고 무덤덤하게 대답했다.

"이혼하고 먹고살 일 생각하면 이건 별로 신경도 안 쓰여. 그냥 혹 떼는 느낌이야."

"그래. 혹은 나도 떼봤는데, 별것 아니더라고."

나는 환자복을 입고 누운 해주를 바라보며 농담을 했다. 해주는 그 말이 재밌다는 듯 깔깔댔다.

"수술은 어땠어?"

"그냥 뭐, 끔찍했지."

해주는 내 대답을 듣고는 물끄러미 나를 올려다봤다.

*

The next day, Haejoo and I took a taxi to the hospital. Haejoo was perfectly calm. In the cab and also as she went up and down the hospital corridor getting all sorts of tests done, she didn't seem particularly nervous. While she was in the recovery room waiting for her surgery, an IV drip in her arm, I asked if she was scared and she answered evenly that she wasn't, not really.

"When I think about how I'm going to make a living after the divorce, this is nothing. Feels like getting a lump removed."

I looked down at Haejoo lying there in her hospital gown and joked, "Yeah. I got a lump removed, too, and it was no big deal." She cackled, amused.

"How was your surgery?"

"Oh, you know—terrible."

At that, Haejoo looked up at me with empty eyes. Then she told me she was sorry she hadn't been there with me, but honestly, it wasn't something for her to be sorry about. I was the one who'd cut off all contact when she said she wanted to see me all transformed. Still, when Haejoo went in for her operation, leaving me alone in the recovery room, I felt grateful that she'd apologized. I never officially

그러고는 그동안 곁에 있지 못해 미안하다고 말했는데, 사실 해주가 사과할 일은 아니었다. 달라진 모습으로 만나자며 일방적으로 연락을 끊은 건 나였으니까. 다만 해주가 수술실로 들어가 혼자 회복실에 남겨졌을 때에는 사과해주어 고맙다는 마음이 되기는 했다. 연락하지 말라고 선언했다고 한들 진짜 전화번호를 차단해놓은 것은 아니었다. 해주가 늦은 밤 전화를 걸어왔다면, 내가 걱정된다고 문자메시지라도 보냈다면, 나는 못 이기는 척 해주를 만났을 것이다. 그리고 어쩔 수 없다는 듯 변해가는 모습을 보여주었을 것이다. 그러나 해주는 그러지 않았고, 나 역시 그제 전화를 걸어온 해주처럼 오랜 친구에게 도움을 청하지 못했다.

　나는 첫 수술을 혼자 치렀다. 혼자서 태국으로 떠났고, 그곳에서 대수술을 받았다. 지금은 수술에 대한 것을 대부분 잊어버렸다. 전신마취에서 깨어나던 순간의 통증이나, 며칠 동안 같은 자세로 누워 천장을 가만히 올려다보던 날들이 이제는 흐릿해졌다. 그나마 또렷이 기억나는 것은 환자식으로 제공되었던 구아바 주스와 호박 스프의 이국적인 맛이다. 장의 일부를 떼어낸 탓에 수술 후 며칠 동안은 오직 액체만 먹을 수 있었는데, 그때 그런 음료들

told her not to call, and I never actually blocked her number. Had she called me late at night, had she messaged me saying she was worried, I would have gone to her—with reservations, but still. I would have gone. And with no other choice, I would have shown her the new me. But that didn't happen, and unlike Haejoo when she'd called me up two days ago, I wasn't able to ask my longtime friend for help.

I underwent my first surgery alone. I went to Thailand by myself, and it was there I had the big operation done. By now, I've forgotten most things about the procedure. The ache I felt upon waking up from the general anesthesia, the days I spent lying still in the same position and staring up at the ceiling, have now become a blur. Yet the one thing I distinctly remember was the exotic taste of the guava juice and pumpkin soup the hospital served. Part of my intestines had been removed during the surgery, so I could only have liquids for the next several days, which was when I had those foods. I straightened up as I drank my meals through a straw. When I lifted my head and took the straw into my mouth, the nurse in charge of feeding me would compliment me, saying I was a "brave lady," and each time I would summon all the strength I had inside me just to give her a thumbs up.

이 나왔다. 나는 그것들을 빨대로 빨아 먹으며 몸을 추슬렀다. 내가 고개를 들어 빨대를 물 때면 식사를 담당하던 간호사가 "브레이브 레이디"라고 칭찬해주곤 했는데, 나는 그때마다 온 힘을 다해 엄지를 들어보였다.

한 시간 남짓한 수술 끝에 다시 회복실로 실려 온 해주는 곤히 잠들어 있었다. 잠시 뒤 일어나서는 가슴이 아프다고 말했는데, 예상치 못한 말이라서 나는 좀 당황했다. 해주는 내 표정을 보더니 웃음을 터뜨렸다.

"아니, 유방통이 있다고." 해주가 침대에 누운 채 말했다. "거긴 건드리지도 않았는데, 왜 그러지."

"간호사한테 물어볼까?"

"아냐, 됐어."

나는 호르몬 문제일지 모른다고, 호르몬 투여를 시작했을 때 내게도 그런 증상이 있었다고 말하려다가 그만뒀다. 그 대신 휴대전화로 임신중절 수술의 후유증을 검색해보았고, 종종 가슴에 통증을 느끼는 사람들이 있다는 문서를 찾아내 읽어주었다.

*

After the surgery, which lasted a little over an hour, Haejoo was brought back into the recovery room, fast asleep. When she woke up a little while later, she said her heart ached, and I was taken aback, not having expected to hear that. Seeing the look on my face, Haejoo burst out laughing.

"No, I mean my breasts," she said, lying down. "They didn't even touch them. I have no idea why they hurt so much."

"Should I ask the nurse?"

"No, it's all right."

I started to tell her it might be a hormonal issue, how I'd had the same symptom when I first started hormones, but I stopped myself. I looked up side effects of abortion on my phone and found an article that said there were occasionally people who experienced chest pains. I read that aloud to her instead.

*

I had played a big part in Haejoo and Minhyung becoming a couple. Minhyung dragged out confessing to her for a long time, and since he was afraid she would turn him down if he asked her to hang out alone, just the two of them, he aggressively begged me to accompany them, an almost pleading look on

해주와 민형이 연인이 된 데에는 나의 공이 제법 컸다. 민형은 해주에게 고백하기까지 시간을 오래도 끌었는데, 단둘이 만나자고 했다가 거절당할 것을 두려워해서 내게 적극적으로, 때로는 거의 절박한 표정으로 동행을 청했다. 나는 될 수 있는 한 민형의 부탁을 들어주었다. 그렇게 나는 해주, 민형과 함께 학교 근처의 식당이며 호프집을 돌아다녔고, 어느 날은 학교 정문에서 명동까지 걸어가 레코드숍을 구경했다.

두 사람이 연인이 되고 나서도 그런 날들은 심심찮게 이어졌다. 특히 영화와 관계된 이벤트에 있어서는, 두 사람은 꼭 내게 동행을 청했다. 우리는 개봉 첫날 서울극장에 가서 〈화양연화〉를 봤고, 내한한 왕가위 감독과 양조위, 장만옥을 보겠다며 피카디리극장 앞에서 한나절을 기다렸다. 우리가 가장 좋아하던 일은 동아리방에서 함께 비디오테이프를 보는 것이었다. 동아리방에 영화를 보는 데 필요한 모든 것이 다 있었으므로 가능했던 일이었다. 당시로서는 화면이 제법 넓었던 텔레비전과 비디오 플레이어, 원래는 3인용이지만 여섯 명은 족히 앉을 수 있는 커다란 소파가 거기 있었다. 방의 한 면을 차지하고 있는 책장에는 선배들이 대대로 모아온 비디오테이프

his face. I did what I could to help him out. That was how I ended up frequenting restaurants and bars near campus with the two of them, and even walking from the school gates over to Myeongdong once to look around a record shop.

Even after they started dating, those kinds of days weren't uncommon. Especially when there was something film-related happening, the two of them would always ask me to tag along. We went to Seoul Cinema to see *In the Mood for Love* the day it was released, and we waited outside the Picadilly Theater for half a day for a chance to see Wong Kar-wai, the director, and Tony Leung and Maggie Cheung, the stars, when they visited Korea. Our favorite thing to do together was watch VHS tapes in the film club room. The club room had everything we could possibly need to screen movies. There was a VHS player and a TV with a screen that was considered huge at the time, as well as a big sofa that was technically a three-seater but could comfortably fit six. One wall of the room was occupied by a bookcase crammed with videotapes collected by generations and generations of upperclassmen, so we could even pick which movie we wanted to watch. On top of that, the collection was steadily growing. That was because Minhyung went around buying up all the tapes

가 빼곡히 꽂혀 있어서, 보고 싶은 영화를 골라 보는 것도 가능했다. 게다가 비디오테이프는 점점 많아졌다. 민형이 폐업 세일을 하는 비디오 가게를 돌아다니며 온갖 비디오를 사 모았기 때문이다. 동성애를 다루었다는 이유로 개봉이 불허되었던 〈해피 투게더〉의 해적판을 구해온 것도 민형이었다. 나는 지금도 품에 비디오테이프를 안은 채 열띤 얼굴을 하고 있던 민형을 기억한다.

"이것 봐."

늦은 오후, 다짜고짜 동아리방으로 나를 불러낸 민형은 인사도 없이 비디오 케이스 하나를 불쑥 내밀었다. 아무것도 적혀 있지 않은 반투명한 케이스였다. 나는 케이스를 열고 테이프 중앙의 라벨에 적힌 글자를 읽었다. HAPPY TOGETHER, 1997, 왕가위. 민형은 놀란 내 표정을 보더니 더욱 신이 나서 말했다.

"해주는 곧 올 거야."

잠시 뒤 해주가 도착하자, 우리는 거의 비장한 마음으로 동아리방의 낡은 소파에 자리를 잡고 앉았다. 두말할 것도 없이 〈해피 투게더〉는 왕가위의 최고작이었다. 그날 우리는 그 자명한 사실을 알게 되었고, 당연하다는 듯 그 자리에서 영화를 처음부터 다시 봤다. 그리고 첫차가

from video store closeout sales. He was the one who'd acquired a bootleg copy of the film *Happy Together*, which had been barred from release because it dealt with homosexuality. Even now, I remember how elated Minhyung had looked hugging that tape to his chest.

One late afternoon, Minhyung called me over to the film club room out of nowhere and, without so much as a hello, thrust a VHS case at me. "Check this out," he said. It was a see-through case with nothing written on it. I opened it and read the words on the label in the center of the tape. HAPPY TO-GETHER, 1997, Wong Kar-wai. Minhyung grew even more excited seeing the surprise on my face.

"Haejoo's on her way," he said.

When she arrived soon after, we took our seats on the worn club room sofa, an almost steely determination in our hearts. Needless to say, *Happy Together* was Wong Kar-wai's best film. We came to know this self-evident truth that day and then, of course, stayed behind and started the movie over from the beginning. We talked about it until the first trains started running. It was a summer day, the cicadas fiercely crying outside and the old electric fan slowly making its turns around the room.

다닐 때까지 영화 이야기를 했다. 창밖에서 매미들이 맹렬하게 울고 낡은 선풍기가 탈탈거리며 돌아가던 여름날이었다.

*

집으로 돌아오는 동안 해주는 이제 수술도 끝났으니 맥주라도 한잔하자고 소리쳤는데, 집에 도착해서는 일찌감치 잠들어버렸다. 나는 혼자 마트에 가서 미역과 관자, 그리고 내가 먹을 과자와 맥주를 잔뜩 샀다. 그리고 해주네 부엌에서 가장 큰 냄비를 찾아 미역을 불리기 시작했다. 그러는 동안 해주는 침실에서 두 팔을 머리 위로 한 채 잠들어 있었다. 밖이 완전히 깜깜해지고 미역국이 다 끓었을 때에도 마찬가지였다. 나는 해주를 깨우는 대신 맥주병을 들고 거실의 소파에 앉았다. 그리고 해주네에서 자주 그랬듯 텔레비전 VOD로 영화를 보기 시작했다. 함께 술을 마실 때면 해주나 민형은 그렇게 영화를 틀어놓곤 했다. 열에 아홉은 왕가위의 영화였다. 집중해서 보지는 않았지만 대화 사이의 배경음으로 광둥어 대사가 흘러들어오는 것을 우리 모두 좋아했다.

On the way home, Haejoo loudly proclaimed that we should at least have a beer now that she was done with the surgery, but when we got back to her apartment, she passed out early. I went to the mart alone and bought some seaweed and scallop meat, plus a ton of snacks and some beer for me to enjoy. I found the biggest pot there was in Haejoo's kitchen and started steeping the seaweed. While I was doing that, Haejoo was in her bedroom, asleep with her arms over her head. The seaweed soup finished cooking right when it had gotten completely dark outside. Rather than wake Haejoo, I grabbed a beer and went to sit on the living room sofa. Just like we often would at her place, I started watching an on-demand movie on TV. When we drank together, Haejoo or Minhyung would always put something on. Nine times out of ten, it was a Wong Kar-wai movie. We never really focused on the film, but we loved having the sounds of Cantonese dialogue flowing through our conversations as background noise.

"What are you doing up?"

Haejoo came into the living room looking all disheveled just as Leslie Cheung and Tony Leung

"안 자고 뭐해?"

해주가 부스스한 얼굴로 거실로 걸어 나온 것은 장국영과 양조위가 재회해, 텔레비전 화면이 흑백에서 컬러로 막 바뀌었을 때였다.

"영화 보려고."

나는 그렇게 대답하고 영화를 정지시킨 다음 해주가 먹을 미역국을 데웠다. 우리는 각자 맥주와 미역국을 먹으며 영화를 보기 시작했다. 미역국을 다 먹은 해주는 내가 마시던 맥주를 뺏어 조금씩 홀짝거렸다. 영화가 끝나갈 즘, 해주가 자신은 더 이상 왕가위의 팬이 아님을 다소 비밀스러운 말투로 털어놓았다.

"로만 폴란스키를 지지했잖아."

해주는 한층 더 조심스럽게 덧붙였다. 나도 뉴스에서 보고 알고 있던 사실이었다. 아동 성범죄를 저지른 그 영화감독에 대해 수많은 영화인들이 지지 성명을 냈는데, 그중에는 왕가위도 있었다. 다만 그 뉴스를 접했을 때 나는 더 이상 누구의 팬도 아니었기에, 조금 허망했을 뿐 특별하게 실망할 것은 없었다. 그런데 해주는 그렇지 않았던 모양이었다. 해주는 곧 로만 폴란스키를 지지한 영화인들에 대해 통탄하기 시작했다. 그 명단에 한때 우리가

reunited, the TV screen changing from grayscale to color.

"Watching a movie," I said, pausing it and getting up to go heat up some of the seaweed soup for her. Once we each had a bowl and a beer, we started watching the movie again. Haejoo, having finished all her soup, grabbed the beer I'd been drinking and took a sip. Near the end of the movie, she confided in me—like it was a secret—that she was no longer a fan of Wong Kar-wai.

"He supported Roman Polanski, you know," she added carefully. I'd also seen that in the news. Numerous directors had signed a petition in support of Polanski, who had raped a child, and Wong Kar-wai was one of them. Still, by the time I heard about it, I had ceased to be a fan of anyone, and so I felt dismayed but not particularly disappointed. It seemed that hadn't been the case for Haejoo, though. Soon, she started grieving the filmmakers who'd come out in support of Roman Polanski. That list of names included nearly every director we had ever loved, and Haejoo couldn't even begin to put the sense of betrayal she felt into words. As she told me this, surprisingly, she began to cry. I stopped the movie. And I realized the person she felt betrayed by, the person she was grieving, wasn't Wong Kar-wai. She was

좋아했던 거의 모든 감독들이 포함되어 있다고, 배신감이 이루 말할 수 없다고. 그렇게 말하면서 해주는 놀랍게도 눈물을 흘렸다. 나는 영화를 멈추었다. 그리고 해주가 이렇게나 배신감을 느끼고 통탄스럽게 여기는 사람이 왕가위가 아님을 깨달았다. 해주는 민형 때문에 울고 있었다.

*

　최근의 민형에 대해서 나는 아는 바가 많지 않다. 오랫동안 몰고 다니던 낡은 소나타를 아내에게 넘겨주고 자신은 새로운 지프차를 뽑았다는 것과, 고혈압을 진단받고 약을 먹기 시작했다는 것 정도를 알고 있는데, 이마저도 해주를 통해 재작년에 혹은 그 이전에 들은 것이다. 밤늦게까지 술을 마시고 영화를 보던 우리의 단출한 파티가 끝나면서 사실상 민형과의 관계도 끊어진 셈이었다. 우리의 파티는 내가 두 사람의 초대를 거듭 거절하며 갑작스레 작파되었다. 나는 처음에 바쁘다는 핑계를 댔고, 그다음에는 이제 술을 좀 끊어보려고 한다고 거짓말을 했다. 사실 그즈음 나는 성전환을 생각하며 그동안 나를

crying over Minhyung.

*

I didn't know much about Minhyung as of late. I knew he'd left the old Sonata he used to drive around to his wife and picked out a brand-new jeep for himself, and that he'd started on a new medication after being diagnosed with hypertension, but even those were things I'd heard via Haejoo the year before last or even longer ago than that. When those simple parties where we'd stay up late drinking and watching movies ended, so did any real relationship I'd had with Minhyung. The parties came to a halt when I refused their invitations over and over. At first, my excuse was that I was busy, and then it was the lie that I had been trying to cut back on my drinking. In reality, I had been thinking about having gender confirmation surgery at the time and was putting some distance between myself and the people who'd long known and accepted me as gay. It seemed like too much of a hassle to meet up and hang out with anyone while I had quit my job and was scraping together the money for the surgery. Even buying wine to drink with them was more than I could afford. But if I had to name one reason as the

게이로 알고 받아들여준 사람들에게 거리를 두고 있었다. 직장을 그만두고 수술비를 마련하느라 누군가와 만나 어울리기가 영 부담스럽기도 했다. 두 사람과 함께 마실 와인을 사는 것마저 사정이 여의치 않았으니까. 그러나 결정적인 이유를 하나 꼽자면 마지막으로 해주네에서 셋이 함께 와인을 마시던 날의 일들 때문이었다. 그날이 다른 날들과 크게 달랐던 것은 아니다. 나는 여느 때처럼 와인 두 병을 사들고 저녁 무렵 해주네 아파트를 찾았고, 해주와 민형은 전골 요리를 준비해놓고 있었다. 우리는 거실 한가운데에 좌탁을 펼쳐놓고 휴대용 가스버너로 전골을 끓였다. 밖은 아직 추워서 베란다 창에 수증기가 서렸는데, 그 덕분에 제법 오붓한 분위기가 연출됐다. 배추와 표고버섯이 흐물흐물해지고 쇠고기가 익어갈 즘 나는 영화를 틀자고 제안했다. 거기에 〈가유희사〉라는 답을 한 사람은 해주였다. 곧 장국영의 기일이니까 그걸 보자고, 장국영의 즐거운 모습이 보고 싶다고 해주는 말했다. 해주의 말처럼 〈가유희사〉에는 장국영의 유쾌한 모습이 많이 나왔다. 영화 속에서 장국영은 여성성을 과장하는 코믹한 남성 캐릭터를 연기했는데, 새된 소리로 별것 아닌 일에 비명을 지르고, 과하게 끼를 부리며 꽃꽂이를 하

determining factor, it would be on account of what happened the last time the three of us drank together at Haejoo's place. It wasn't as if that day had been much different from other days. Just as I had all the other times, I bought two bottles of wine and went over to Haejoo's around the start of the evening, when she and Minhyung were preparing the ingredients for jeongol. We set up the floor table in the middle of the living room and cooked the hot pot over a portable gas burner. It was still cold outside, so the steam fogged up the balcony windows, creating a fairly homey atmosphere. Right as the cabbage and shiitake mushrooms were getting soft and the beef was almost cooked, I suggested we put on a movie. Haejoo was the one who mentioned *All's Well, Ends Well*. The anniversary of Leslie Cheung's death was coming up, and she wanted us to watch something that showed him happy. Like she said, you got to see a lot of Leslie Cheung's sunny side in *All's Well, Ends Well*. In the movie, Cheung plays a comical male character who lays his femininity on thick, squealing at the slightest provocation and flirting excessively while he arranges flowers. It was a typical Hong Kong B-movie and wasn't even all that entertaining or funny, but it was the perfect background to have on while we were having a meal. Immersed

는 식이었다. 전형적인 B급 홍콩영화였고 그리 재미있지도 웃기지도 않았지만, 뭔가 먹고 마시면서 배경으로 틀어놓기에는 아주 맞춤했다. 우리는 한창 다른 얘기를 하다가 화면으로 눈을 돌려 킬킬댔고, 그러다 다시 무언가를 먹고 마셨다. 그 흐름을 깬 것은 민형이었다. 민형은 화면 속에서 원피스 잠옷을 입은 장국영을 보고 갑자기 폭소를 터뜨렸는데, 사실 거기에는 그렇게나 우스울 것이 없었다. 적어도 나와 해주의 눈에는 그랬다. 잠시 뒤 웃음을 그친 민형은 조금 멋쩍어하며 '저런 영화'가 장국영의 커리어를 망쳤다고 다소 뜬금없는 얘기를 꺼냈다. 그러니까 80~90년대 홍콩 영화계에는 좋은 영화감독이 절대적으로 부족해서, 장국영은 저런 영화를 찍는 데 시간을 허비해야 했다는 것이 민형의 요지였다.

"재밌는데, 왜? 그리고 귀엽잖아."

나는 민형의 말에 해주가 기분이 상했을 거라고 생각해 그렇게 말했다. 돌이켜보면 그즈음에 민형은 자주 그런 태도로 해주를 기분 나쁘게 하곤 했다. 셋이 함께 있을 때 장난스럽게 해주의 취향을 놀렸고, 직장을 그만두고 온종일 집에 있는 해주가 부럽다고 말하는 식이었다.

"너네는 재밌겠지. 장국영 팬이니까." 민형은 다시 말

in a conversation about something else, we would turn to the screen and chuckle, then pick up eating and drinking again. Minhyung was the one who disrupted our flow. At the sight of Leslie Cheung wearing a nightgown onscreen, he suddenly howled with laughter, though there really wasn't anything that hilarious about it. At least, not to Haejoo and me. After a moment, Minhyung stopped laughing, looking sheepish, but then he said sort of out of nowhere that doing "that kind of movie" was what had tanked Leslie Cheung's career. His point, he said, was that there had been a dearth of good directors in the Hong Kong film world in the 80s and 90s, so Cheung had been left to waste his talents starring in these sorts of films.

"So what, if it's funny?" I said. "Plus, he's cute, isn't he?" I thought Haejoo might have been offended by what Minhyung said. Looking back on it, Minhyung would often ruin Haejoo's mood with that sort of behavior back then. When the three of us were together, he would tease her about her tastes, then tell her he envied her for quitting her job and sitting around the house all day.

"Of course it's funny to you," Minhyung said. "You're his fan. But that's how I see it. He didn't have to be such a sissy."

했다. "그렇지만 내 생각은 그래. 저렇게 쪼다가 될 필요는 없었다는 거지."

화면 속에서 과하게 볼터치 분장을 한 장국영을 보고 한 말이었다. 이후 나는 해주 부부와 한동안 거리를 두고 지냈다. 민형이 한 말이 내게 모욕적이라고 생각하기도 했고, 민형이 너무 변했다고 느꼈던 것도 같다. 복사판 〈해피 투게더〉 비디오를 공수해 오고, 장국영이 죽었다는 소식을 조심스럽게 전해주었던 내 친구는 어디론가 증발해버렸다고 생각했다.

다만 해주와는 종종 단둘이 만나곤 했다. 우리는 주로 광화문이나 시청에서 만나 저녁을 먹고 헤어졌다.

*

다음 날, 아침을 먹는 내내 해주는 오늘 무얼 할지에 대해 떠들어댔다. 근처에 오픈한 대형 쇼핑몰을 구경하고, 극장에 들러 영화를 한 편 본 다음, 저녁에는 예전처럼 와인을 한잔 마시자고 해주는 말했다. 마치 내가 이 집에 놀러와 있고, 자신은 친구를 재미있게 해줘야 할 의무가 있다는 듯한 태도였다.

As he said this, Leslie Cheung was onscreen emphatically applying rouge to his cheeks.

After that, I distanced myself from them as a couple for a while. I thought Minhyung had been targeting me with what he'd said. He had changed too much. It was like my friend—the one who'd had that copy of *Happy Together* airmailed in, who'd carefully broken the news to me when Leslie Cheung died—had somehow evaporated, vanished into thin air.

I would still see Haejoo, just the two of us, from time to time. We'd meet up mostly around Gwanghwamun or City Hall, have dinner together, then go our separate ways.

*

The next morning, all through breakfast, Haejoo went on and on about what to do that day. We should go and have a look around the huge shopping mall that just opened up nearby, she said, then stop by the movie theater to catch a show and have some wine for dinner like we would in the old days. Just as I thought, I'd come over to her house and now she was acting as if she had an obligation to entertain me.

"I mean, it's fine if we don't do all that," was all I

"글쎄, 꼭 그러지 않아도 돼."

나는 코로나 바이러스니, 당분간 쉬어야 한다느니 하는 말 대신 그렇게만 대꾸했다. 해주는 자신을 보살피러 온 나에게조차 아무렇지 않게 보이고 싶어 하는 것 같았다. 아침 밥상에서 어젯밤의 일을 한마디도 꺼내지 않은 것부터가 그랬다. 사실 우리는 그런 점이 비슷했다. 그리고 바로 그런 이유에서, 나는 해주의 부름을 의뭉스럽게 생각하기도 했다. 나와 달리 해주는 친구가 많았는데, 내가 알기로 그들은 모두 결혼해 자녀를 두고 있었다. 어쩌면 해주는 그들에게 간호받길 원치 않았을지도 몰랐다. 사실 나는 이런 의심을 제법 오랫동안, 그러니까 해주와 민형이 내게 딩크족 부부의 탄생을 축하해달라고 말했을 때부터 품어왔다. 해주 부부가 아이를 포기하겠다고 선언했던 시점에 이미 나는 게이라고 커밍아웃을 했던 터였으므로, 내가 가정을 꾸리고 자녀를 둘 가능성이 전혀 없다는 것을 두 사람은 알고 있었다.

그 사실이 우리의 잦은 만남에 영향을 미쳤을지 모른다고 종종 생각했다. 술에 취해 해주네의 작은 방에 마련된 1인용 침대에 몸을 누일 때면, 한순간에 취기가 가시며 그런 생각이 찾아왔다.

said instead of what I'd wanted to say, which was that we should rest for the time being on account of the coronavirus. I had come here to take care of her, but Haejoo seemed to want to make it look as though none of this were a big deal. For one thing, she hadn't said a word about what had happened last night since we sat down at the breakfast table. Honestly, the two of us were similar in that way. And that was exactly why I began to think there was an underlying motive to her having called me. Unlike me, Haejoo had a ton of friends, but as far as I knew, all of them were married with kids. Maybe she hadn't wanted them nursing her back to health. In fact, I'd harbored these sorts of doubts for a long time, ever since Haejoo and Minhyung asked me to celebrate the birth of their DINK coupledom with them. By the time they announced they were giving up on having a baby, I had already come out as gay, so the two of them had known there was absolutely no chance of me starting a family and having any kids.

From time to time, I wondered whether that fact had any bearing on our frequent gatherings. Lying drunk on the single bed in Haejoo's guest room, I would sober up at once when that thought crossed my mind.

"아니면 드라이브라도 다녀오자."

해주가 다시 말했다. 한강 옆으로 난 도로를 달리다가, 드라이브스루 카페에 들러 음료를 포장해 오자는 계획이었다. 곧 우리는 외출 준비를 했다. 해주가 운전대를 잡았다. 탁 트인 8차선 도로에 이르러 해주는 점차 속력을 높였고, 그러자 자동차 천장에서 탈탈거리는 소리가 났다. 자갈 같은 것이 천장 위를 대굴대굴 굴러다니는 소리였다. 해주는 카센터에 가서 점검을 받았으나, 별 이상은 없었다고 나를 안심시켰다. 수술 이후 무언가 달라진 것이 있냐고 물은 것은 그다음이었다. 그때서야 나는 이틀 밤을 함께 보내는 동안 해주가 나에 대해 자세한 근황을 묻지 않았다는 사실을 깨달았다.

"글쎄, 뭐 보면 알잖아." 나는 여름용 주름치마를 입고 있는 내 모습을 내려다보며 말했다. "나쁘지 않지. 적어도 입고 싶은 옷을 입을 순 있으니까."

차창 밖으로 여름 볕을 받은 개천이 보였다. 우리는 양수리 쪽으로 달려가는 중이었다.

"그럼 다행이고."

해주는 전방에 시선을 고정한 채 말했다.

어쩌면 해주는 일부러 이 공간을 선택했는지도 몰랐

"Or let's go for a drive," said Haejoo. Her plan was for us to take the road that ran alongside the Han River and get some drinks to go from a drive-thru cafe. Soon, we were ready to go out. Haejoo took the wheel. As we came to the wide-open eight-lane highway, Haejoo gradually began to accelerate, which was when we heard a clattering sound coming from the roof, like pebbles or something rolling over the top of the car. Haejoo went to the auto center for an inspection, and I was flooded with relief when she told me there were no issues with the car. The next thing I knew, she was asking me whether anything had changed for me after my surgery. I realized then that in the two nights I had spent with her, she hadn't once asked me in detail how I'd been.

"Well, you can see for yourself," I said, looking down at myself in the pleated summer skirt I was wearing. "Not bad, right? I can at least wear what I want now."

Outside the window, I could see a creek glittering in the summer sun. We were headed toward Yangsu-ri.

"That's a relief," Haejoo said, her eyes fixed on the road ahead.

I thought she might have chosen this place on

다. 나란히 앉아 마주보지 않아도 되고, 시선을 둘 곳이 정해져 있으니까. 해주와 마지막으로 만났던 날, 바로 이 차에서 나는 해주에게 당분간은 연락이 어려울 거라는 말을 꺼냈다. 달라진 모습에 적응하게 되면 그때 만나자고, 길어야 1년일 거라고. 물론 내 생각보다 그 시기는 길었고 해주의 전화가 아니었다면 영영 만나지 않았을지도 모르지만. 나는 삼십대 중반에야 성전환을 결심한 드문 케이스였다. 오래전에 나는 스스로를 평범한 사람이라고 믿고 싶어 했고, 그러다 게이라는 정체성으로 겨우 타협을 봤다. 나는 그 믿음을 유지하기 위해 해주와 민형을 비롯한 주변 사람들에게 커밍아웃을 시작했는데, 돌이켜보면 그건 일종의 자기 학대였다.

"내가 보기엔, 더 좋아 보여."

해주가 또 말했다.

"맞아. 더 편해졌어, 여러 가지로."

나는 차창 너머로 흘러드는 풀 냄새를 맡으며 그렇게 말했다. 어느새 도로 옆으로 호수가 보이기 시작했다. 카페 근처까지 다다랐을 때는 오후 3시가 넘어갈 즘이었다. 드라이브스루 매대로 들어가는 자동차들의 줄은 카페 밖의 도로까지 뻗어 나와 있었다. 해주는 비상등을 켠 채 그

purpose. So we could sit side by side without facing each other, the places where our gazes could fall having already been decided. The day I had met up with Haejoo for the last time, in this very same car, I told her it would be hard for me to contact her for a while. I said we should meet up again once I had adjusted to my new body, which would take a year at most. Of course, the actual time that lapsed was longer than I'd expected. Had it not been for her calling me, who knows? We may have never seen each other again. As someone who had decided to undergo gender confirmation surgery in their mid-thirties, I was a rare case. A long time ago, I'd wanted to believe I was an average person, and I had just barely managed to find a compromise in a gay identity. To maintain that belief, I'd begun coming out to the people around me, starting with Haejoo and Minhyung. But looking back on it, I can see that was a kind of self-harm.

"If you ask me, you look better," Haejoo said.

"Yeah," I said, breathing in the smell of grass coursing in through the window. "I've gotten more comfortable in a lot of ways."

Before I knew it, a lake came into view on the side of the road. When we got to the cafe, it was a little past 3 p.m. The line of cars queued up at the

줄의 끝에 차를 댔다. 매대로 진입하는 차들은 아주 천천히 움직여서, 여기서 한 시간쯤은 우습게 지날 수도 있겠다는 생각이 들었다. 그리고 해주도 같은 생각을 했는지, 아예 카페로 들어가서 커피를 마시는 것은 어떻겠느냐고 내게 물었다. 2층의 야외 테라스 자리에 앉으면 그리 위험하지도 않고, 호수를 내려다볼 수 있다고 말이다. 과연 그렇게 보이기는 했다. 푸른 파라솔 아래에서 사람들이 아이스 커피를 마시는 풍경이 좋아 보였다. 다만 나는 그러길 원치 않았는데, 이태원 의외의 공간에서 치마를 입고 돌아다니는 일은 아무래도 꺼려졌기 때문이다. 사실 호르몬 치료에 앞서 해방촌으로 이사부터 한 이유가 그것이었다. 해주네 아파트에서처럼 마트에 다녀오기 위해 모자를 쓰고 매니큐어를 지우지 않아도 됐으니까. 그러나 그런 사정을 설명하면서 저기에 가고 싶지 않다고 말하기는 어려웠으므로 나는 그저 코로나 바이러스를 핑계 댔다. 아무래도 위험할 것 같다고, 저 사람들을 좀 보라고, 마스크를 벗고 있다고.

"아무래도 그렇겠지?"

해주는 내 말에 고개를 끄덕거렸다. 우리는 거의 한 시간을 기다려 스무디 두 잔을 받아 들었다. 돌아오는 동

drive-thru menu stretched out to the road. Haejoo cut on her hazard lights and parked at the end of the line. The cars were moving through the line very slowly, and I had a funny feeling we might be there for an hour or so. Haejoo seemed to be thinking the same and asked how I felt about just going into the cafe and having our drinks inside. She said it wouldn't be dangerous if we sat on the outdoor terrace on the second floor, and from there, we'd be able to look out over the lake. That seemed feasible enough. The view of people sitting beneath blue parasols and drinking iced coffees was pleasant. Even so, I didn't want to go in, still somewhat reluctant to walk around in a skirt outside of Itaewon. That was one reason I'd moved to Haebangchon before starting hormones. Because there, unlike at Haejoo's apartment, I didn't have to put on a hat or remove my nail polish to go to the mart. But knowing it would be too hard to explain that I didn't want to go inside for that sort of reason, I just used the coronavirus as an excuse. *Still, it seems sort of risky, I mean, look at those people, they're taking off their masks.*

"I guess you're right," said Haejoo, nodding.

We waited almost an hour to get our two smoothies. On the drive back, we listened to the whole

안에는 '캘리보니아 드리밍'부터 시작해 〈중경삼림〉의 OST를 모조리 들었고, 대학 시절 연인으로 오해받던 일을 얘기하며 킬킬댔다. 나는 민형보다 먼저 해주와 가까워졌는데, 동아리 선배들은 해주와 내가 자주 붙어 다니는 것을 보고 당연히 캠퍼스커플이려니 생각했다. 그러다 해주와 민형이 연인이 되자 모두들 놀라워했다. 아마도 민형이 내게서 해주를 빼앗아갔다고 생각하는 눈치였다. 우리는 그 상황을 재미있어 해서, 민형과 셋이 어울리던 시절에는 질리지도 않고 그 얘기를 하고 또 했다.

*

그렇게 수다를 떨다가 집에 도착했을 때에는 놀랍게도 민형이 우리보다 먼저 집에 와 있었다. 그는 거실의 소파에 앉아 있었고, 해주를 뒤따라 집에 들어온 나를 단번에 알아보지 못했다. 몇 초 뒤 민형은 거의 신음에 가까운 한숨을 내쉬며 나를 훑어보았다. 아내와 무언가 얘기를 나눠야 한다는 생각조차 잊어버린 듯했다. 나 역시 멍해진 채 옛 친구를 바라보고 서 있었는데, 해주가 가장 먼저 정신을 차리고 상황을 정리했다. 해주는 남편의 손을 잡아

Chungking Express soundtrack starting from "California Dreaming" and laughed out loud as we reminisced on the times in college when we'd been mistaken for a couple. I was close with Haejoo before Minyung was, and our film club seniors often saw us together and naturally thought we were a campus couple. Everyone was shocked when Haejoo and Minhyung started going out. They probably assumed he had stolen her from me. We thought it was the funniest thing and told that story over and over, never tiring of the days we used to spend, the three of us, together.

*

When we got back to Haejoo's place after chatting like that for a while, we were surprised to see that Minhyung had beaten us there. He was sitting on the living room sofa and didn't immediately recognize me when I came trailing in behind Haejoo. After several seconds, Minhyung let out a sigh that was almost a groan as he looked me over. It was like he completely forgot what he'd needed to talk to his wife about. While I stood there staring blankly as ever at my old friend, Haejoo was the first one to pull herself together and sort the situation out.

끌어 민형을 안방으로 들여보냈고, 내게는 민형과 이야기를 나눌 동안만 작은방에 있어달라고 부탁했다. 나는 그때서야 정신이 들어 자리를 피해주겠다고 말하고 집에서 나갔다. 두 사람에게는 시간이 필요하고, 아무래도 내가 있으면 불편할 테니까. 다만 집 밖에서 있을 곳이 마땅찮았으므로, 나는 그저 해주네 아파트 단지를 천천히 돌기 시작했다. 단지는 넓었고, 걸을 때마다 연분홍색 주름치마가 스치며 부스럭거려서 내가 치마를 입고 있다는 사실을 끝도 없이 상기시켰다. 선선한 저녁이었다. 하늘은 천천히 어두워졌고 때때로 미풍이 불어왔다. 나는 해주와 민형이 지금쯤 어떤 이야기를 나눌지 상상해봤다. 민형이 사과했을지, 만약 그랬다면 해주가 민형을 용서했을지 궁금해졌다. 나는 해주가 그러지 않기를 바랐다. 그 편이 해주에게 좋다고 생각했다. 사실 내게도 그랬다. 나는 언제나 해주의 불행을 반가워했다. 해주가 임신이 어려운 몸이라는 말을 들었을 때, 임신을 완전히 포기하겠다고 선언했을 때, 그리고 민형과 이혼하겠다고 며칠 전 얘기했을 때, 그때마다 나는 해주가 조금 더 마이너한 사람이 되어주길 바랐다. 해주가 아이를 낳지 않기를 은밀하게 원했고, 홀로 되어 우리가 좀 더 많은 것을 공유할

She took her husband's hand and led him into their bedroom, then asked me to wait in the guest room while she and Minhyung talked. It was only then that I came to my senses and told her I would step out for a bit, give them some space. Then I left. The two of them needed time, and it would only be uncomfortable for them if I were there. But once I was outside, I had nowhere to go, and so I started slowly circling Haejoo's apartment complex. It was huge, and with each step I took, my light pink pleated skirt rustled and swished, making me acutely aware of the fact that I was wearing it. It was a cool evening. The sky was slowly darkening, and a gentle breeze went by from time to time. I tried to imagine what Haejoo and Minhyung would be talking about right now. I wondered whether Minhyung had apologized, and if he had, whether Haejoo had forgiven him. I hoped she wouldn't. I thought that would be the best thing for her. And to be honest, for me, too. I had always delighted in Haejoo's misfortune. When I heard how hard it had been for her to get pregnant, when she announced she was giving up on trying to conceive once and for all, and just a couple days ago when she told me she and Minhyung were getting a divorce—each time, I hoped these misfortunes might push her further and further into the margins.

수 있게 되기를 기대했다. 해주는 나의 유일한 친구였으
니까. 그리고 그런 생각에 빠져 있을 즘, 해주가 내게 전
화를 걸어왔다. 내게 어디냐고 묻고, 데리러 오겠다고 해
주는 말했다. 그러나 아파트 단지의 어디쯤일 뿐, 내가 있
는 곳을 설명하기가 어려웠으므로, 나는 그저 네게서 그
리 멀지 않은 곳에 있다고만 대답했다.

I secretly wanted for her not to have a baby and hoped being all alone would be yet another thing we shared. Because Haejoo was the only friend I had.

Right as I was taken by that thought, Haejoo called me. She asked where I was, said she would come get me. But it would have been too hard to explain my location, that I was just somewhere around the apartment complex, so all I said was, I'm close by, not too far from where you are.

작가노트
Author's Note

「해피 투게더」는 처음 구상했을 때 내가 생각했던 결말은 지금의 소설보다 조금 더 다정하고 작위적인 버전이었다. 처음에 나는 소설 속의 화자가 아파트 단지를 걷다가 다시 해주네 집으로 돌아가게 할 작정이었다. 그리고 셋이 함께 영화 〈해피 투게더〉를 보는 것으로 소설을 마무리 지으려 했다. 세 사람이 잠시나마 'happy together'한 시간을 가졌으면 하는 바람에서였다. 그러나 나중에는 결말을 바꿀 수밖에 없었는데, 화자가 해주의 집으로 돌아간다고 한들 세 사람이 함께 영화를 보지는 않겠다는 걸 쓰는 동안 깨달았기 때문이다.

When I first mapped out "Happy Together," the ending I imagined was a slightly warmer, more contrived version of the current one. At first, I'd planned for the narrator to walk around the apartment complex, then go back to Haejoo's place. And the story would end with the three of them watching the film *Happy Together*. I had hoped they all would be "happy together" in that moment, however briefly. But I later had no choice but to change the ending, because I realized while I was writing that even if the narrator went back to Haejoo's house, there was no way the three of them would watch a movie together.

그러니까 이 소설은 커다란 소파에 나란히 앉아 영화를 보던 친구들이 그 소파를 떠나는 이야기다. 조금 더 정확히 화자의 시점에서 말하자면, 친구들이 모두 소파를 떠날 때까지 소파에 남아 있다가 결국 불 꺼진 스크린 속 자신을 보게 되는 이야기다.

여기까지 쓰고 나니, 초고를 완성하고 나서 걱정했던 문제점 중 하나가 퇴고 과정에서 자연스럽게 사라졌다는 것이 기억난다. 나는 화자가 친구들의 이야기만 전해주는 전달자 역할을 하고 있는 것은 아닌지 한동안 고민했다. 다만 소설을 다듬는 동안 화자가 최선을 다해서 자신의 이야기를 하고 있다고 생각했다. 친구들에 대해서, 그 친구들이 어떻게 사랑하고 싸우고 미워하게 됐는지를 말해주는 것이 그녀가 자신에 대해 최대한으로 이야기하는 방식임을 깨달은 것이다.

물론, 그보다 조금 더 수다스러운 화자가 등장해야 했을지도 모른다. 바로 그 점 때문에 나는 여전히 이 소설이 최선의 방식으로 쓰이지 못했다고 생각하기도 한다. 최선의 방식으로 쓰이지 않은 소설을 이렇게 세상에 내놓아도 되는 것일지, 그것도 한 편의 단편소설을 한 권의 책으로 만드는 프로젝트에 참여해도 될지 걱정이 된다.

And so this is a story about friends who once watched movies side by side on a big sofa getting up from that sofa. More precisely, from the narrator's point of view, this is a story about staying on the sofa until your friends have all gotten up, until the screen eventually cuts to black, allowing you to see yourself in it.

After I'd written up to that point and the draft was complete, I remember one of the trouble spots I'd agonized over naturally disappearing in the process of revision. I worried for a while whether the narrator was simply acting as a messenger for her friends' story. But as I fine-tuned the piece, it seemed to me the narrator was doing her best to tell her own. I realized that talking about her friends, how they had loved and fought and grown to hate one another, was the best medium the narrator had for talking about herself.

Of course, perhaps I could have featured a narrator who was a bit more forthcoming. That itself is one of the reasons I still feel I haven't found the best way to write this story. I worry now about whether it's acceptable to release into the world a story that may not have been told in the best way, as well as to participate in the project of having that single story made into a book. But at the same time, I think it

그러나 지금의 화자가 아닌 다른 화자를 만나는 것은 내 영역 밖의 일이라고도 동시에 생각한다.

would be well beyond my ability to write a narrator other than the one who tells this story now.

해설
Commentary

"네게서 그리 멀지 않은 곳"의 반란

오혜진(문학평론가)

   서장원의 초기작 「주례」(『문학3』 8, 2019. 5)는 존경받는 교사였던 중년 남자 '경묵'의 자아상이 마구 흔들리는 어느 날의 이야기다. '경묵'으로 상징되는 '꼰대'의 몰락은 통쾌하면서도 씁쓸하다. 이처럼 '완고하고 무지한 어른'의 자기보존적 욕망을 불현듯 심문에 부치는 서사는 이 작가의 특기인 듯하다. 다만 그 '완고한 무지'의 대가로, 「주례」의 경묵이 제자의 존경에 담긴 진정성을 의심하게 되는 데 그쳤다면, 후속작들은 한층 더 무참하다. 「해가 지기 전에」(『동아일보』, 2020. 1. 1)·「해변의 밤」(『작가들』 73, 2020년 여름)·「이 인용 게임」(『문학동네』, 2020년 여름)·「이류」(『스마트소설』 1, 문학나무, 2020. 8)에 등장하는 부/모는

A Rebellion "Not Too Far From Where You Are"

Oh Hye-jin(Literary Critic)

One of Seo Jang-won's early works, "Jurye," is the story of one day that rattles the self-image of a respected, middle-aged man and professor, Kyungmook. The downfall of such "boomers" as represented by Kyungmook is satisfying yet bitter. Narratives that suddenly interrogate this desire for self-preservation among "obdurate, ignorant adults" are one of this writer's specialties. Still, while Kyungmook merely ends up doubting the sincerity of his students' respect as a result of that "obdurate ignorance," the author's subsequent stories are harsher in their outcomes. In "Before Sunset," "Nights at the Beach," "Two-Player Game," and "Departure," it is not until fathers/mothers lose their precious sons

귀애하던 아들을 잃고서야 비로소 자신의 '아들 사랑' 방식이 뭔가 잘못됐음을 깨닫는다(혹은 깨닫지 못한다).

요컨대, 이 작가는 타인에 대한 일방적이고 피상적인 사랑만을 고집하는 이들에게는 마치 처벌이나 복수처럼 반드시 '소중한 사람의 상실'이라는 잔혹한 대가를 치르게 한다. 이들에게는 '좋은' 단편소설의 미덕, 즉 "돌이킬 수 없는 지점을 통과하며 예전의 자신과는 다른 사람"[1]이 될 기회조차 좀처럼 부여되지 않는다. 「해변의 밤」의 '나'가 개/아들을 (두 번) 잃고도 여전히 개의 이름을 기억하지 못하듯, 또는 「이 인용 게임」의 '어머니'가 아들만을 향한 배타적인 사랑을 끝내 철회하지 못하듯, 작가는 인간의 변화 가능성을 섣불리 낙관하지 않는다. 그저 그 맹목적인 사람들이 조금 '흔들리는' 순간을 가만히 써둘 뿐이다.

드라마틱한 엔딩이 없는 서장원 소설에서 주목되는 것은 어떤 '소요(逍遙)' 혹은 '유예'의 시간이다. 전 남자친구와 함께 키우던 개를 떠맡은 후, 그가 현재의 아내와 몇 번이고 걸었을 그의 아파트 주변을 빙 돌아보는 시간(「망원」, 『현대문학』784, 2020. 4), 의붓딸을 받아들이거나 아니면 '이혼'이라는 선택지 앞에서 분연히 마음을 정한 후

1. 서장원, 「인생은 바라던 대로 흘러가지 않겠지만」, 『릿터』 26, 2020. 10, 212쪽.

that they come (or fail) to realize there is something wrong with the way in which they show affection for them.

In short, the writer makes those who persist in their shallow, one-sided love for others pay a steep price—"the loss of a loved one"—as a kind of punishment or revenge. Characters are seldom granted the merit of a "nice" short story—that is, the opportunity to "surpass that irreversible point and become someone different than the person you once were."[1] The writer is not heedlessly optimistic about the possibility that human beings can change, whether it's the "I" in "Nights at the Beach" losing their dog/son (twice) and still not being able to remember its name, or the "mother" in "Two-Player Game" being unable until the very end to scale back her insular love for her son. Seo merely puts the moments in which these obtuse people are slightly "rattled" down on paper.

What is noteworthy in Seo's stories, which conclude sans dramatic endings, is the sort of "meandering" or "suspension" of time in them. The time a character spends circling the neighborhood surrounding his apartment with his current wife after taking in the dog he'd raised together with his

1. Seo Jang-won, "Life Won't Go As You'd Hoped, and Yet," *Littor*, Issue 26, October 2020, p. 212.

"어서 태풍이 다가와 주기를" 기다리는 시간(「태풍을 기다리는 저녁」, 웹진 〈문장〉, 2020. 8), 발바닥에 박힌 상상의 가시를 가짜로 뽑아내 잠시 마음의 평온을 구하듯, 어딘가 "여기보다 더 친절한 세계"가 있다는 단꿈을 조금 더 연장하고 싶은 트랜스젠더 게이 커플의 시간(「프랑스 영화처럼」, 웹진 〈비유〉 30, 2020. 6). 의미심장한 유보 같기도, 어차피 정해진 사태의 잉여 같기도 한 이런 순간들을 슬쩍 부려놓은 채, 소설은 멈춘다. 이 의도적인 지연은 서장원 소설의 템포와 텐션을 조절하는 핵심장치이자, 그의 인물들에게 주어지는 마지막 숨고르기의 시간이다. 이 시간의 질감을 헤아려보는 것이야말로 서장원의 독자에게 요청되는 가장 치열한 윤리라고 해도 좋겠다.

「해피 투게더」 또한 신중하게 통제된 서사의 완급이 돋보인다. 한 신문기사는 여성과 트랜스젠더는 모두 "몸에 대한 자기결정권과 재생산권과 가족구성권"이 결여된 존재이며, 이 소설은 그 점을 매개로 한 "'마이너한' 존재들의 우정"[2]을 묘사했다고 썼다. 과연 그런가.

대학 영화 동아리에서 친해진 '나'와 '해주'와 '민형'.

2. 한소범, 「낙태 여성과 트랜스젠더, '마이너한' 존재들의 우정」, 『한국일보』, 2020. 11. 10.

ex-boyfriend ("Mangwon"), the time spent waiting "for the typhoon to come fast" after facing the bold choice of whether to accept one's stepdaughter or get a divorce ("That Evening, Waiting for the Typhoon"), or the time a gay transgender couple wants to prolong that much longer their sweet dream of "a world that is friendlier than here," plucking imaginary thorns from the soles of their feet in search of a brief respite ("Like a French Film"). Under the nimble spell of these moments that feel like weighted pauses and also like a kind of surplus spilling over the bounds of these situations, the stories end. This intentional deferral is the key mechanism regulating the tempo and tension of Seo's stories, the time he allots his characters to catch their breath. It can be said that a keen sense of morality is needed from Seo's readers for the very act of trying to grasp the texture of this time.

The pace of that carefully controlled narration can also be seen in "Happy Together." One newspaper article wrote that women and transgender people all "exist without the right to self-determine, reproduce, or plan their families," and that the story iterates this point through the medium of a "friendship between those living marginal existences."[2] Indeed,

---

2. Han So-beom, "Abortion and Transgender Identity, A Friendship Between 'Minor' Women," *Hankook Ilbo*, November 10, 2020.

어느 날, '나'는 격조했던 해주의 연락을 받는다. 해주가 남편 민형과 이혼할 것이며 곧 임신중절수술을 받으리라는 소식. '나'는 해주 집에 일주일쯤 머물며 해주를 돌봐주기로 한다. 해주를 만나는 것은 '나'가 태국에서 성전환수술을 받은 후 처음이다.

소설은 '나'와 해주의 관계 및 연합의 조건을 공들여 묘사한다. 해주가 집에 들어서자마자 민형의 옷가지를 치우며 "다음에 오면 들려 보내려고."라고 '나'에게 "변명하는 것 같은 말투"로 말하는 장면부터 그렇다. 이는 '나'와 해주의 연합에 필요한 첫 번째 조건이 '나-해주-민형'의 관계에서 민형을 밀어내는 것임을 시사한다. 해주와 민형은 아이를 갖기 위한 노력이 거듭 실패하자 "딩크족 부부"가 되기로 했었다. 그런데 해주가 임신하자, 양육의 고됨을 토로하는 해주와 달리, 민형은 "자신은 아이 없는 삶에 만족한 적이 없다"며 해주의 임신을 "오래 기다린 축복"이라고 말했다는 것이다. 두말할 것 없이, 해주와 '나'는 모두 민형의 말을 "폭언"이자 "실언"으로 여긴다. 즉 이 장면에서 '나'와 해주의 감정적 연대가 성립하고, 독자도 '나-해주'와 '민형' 중 동일시 대상을 택하게 된다. 민형이 종종 해주의 영화 취향을 무시했다거나, "가

it does.

The narrator "I," Haejoo, and Minhyung grew close in a college film club. One day, the narrator receives a call from Haejoo after the two haven't been in touch for a while. With it comes the news that Haejoo and Minhyung, now her husband, are divorcing, and that Haejoo is set to have an abortion. The narrator decides to spend a week or so at Haejoo's house looking after her. It is the first time the narrator is seeing Haejoo after having undergone gender affirmation surgery in Thailand.

The story takes great care to describe the conditions of the alliance that is Haejoo and the narrator's relationship. This is true in the scene where, as soon as Haejoo gets home, she gathers up Minhyung's clothes "so [she] can send them off with him next time he comes by," to which the narrator muses that she "seemed a little like she was making excuses." It is implied that Minhyung has been pushed out of the "narrator-Haejoo-Minhyung" relationship. Having failed repeatedly in their efforts to have a baby, Haejoo and Minhyung have decided to become a "DINK couple." But when Haejoo becomes pregnant, Minhyung—unlike Haejoo, who expresses her worries about the arduous labor of child rearing—has declared that he has "never once been happy

정주부가 되어 온종일 집에 있는 해주가 부럽다"고 말했다는 정보는 민형의 여성혐오를 부각시키며 독자를 '나-해주'로 재현되는 상상의 네트워크에 이입하게 만든다.

이어, 해주는 "너랑 이런 얘길 하는 게 더 편해진 느낌이야. 물론 전에도 그랬지만."이라고 덧붙임으로써 둘의 연합에 필요한 또 하나의 조건을 암시한다. 앞서 '나'와 해주의 연합이 민형의 여성혐오에 대해 함께 분노하는 것으로 충분했다면, 해주의 이 말은 명백히 게이 남성으로 살아가던 '나'가 성전환수술을 받았다는 점을 지시한다. 즉 이 장면에서 '나'와 해주는 서로가, 아니, 해주가 '나'를 ('수술'이라는 의료적 조치를 필수적으로 경유함으로써만 확보되는 신체적 동질성의 약호인) '여성'으로 식별함으로써 "막 한패가 된 악당들처럼 낄낄"댈 수 있었다(이때 마치 중세미술에서 숭고한 인물의 머리 위에 후광을 씌우듯, 식탁 위 노란 전등 불빛이 해주의 머리 위에 "금빛 테두리"를 만들었다는 점을 기억해두자).

하지만 "악당들"의 연합은 잠정적이다. 이를테면, 임신중절수술을 받은 해주는 "유방통"을 호소하는데, 이를 이해할 수 없는 '나'는 "당황"한다. 해주는 그런 '나'를 보며 웃음을 터뜨린다. 즉 소설은 시스젠더 여성인 해주만 웃

being childless" and says of Haejoo's pregnancy that it is "a long-awaited blessing." Needless to say, Haejoo and the narrator respectively regard Minhyung's words as abuses and slips of the tongue. In this scene, the narrator and Haejoo establish an emotional alliance, and the readers, too, choose sides between "the narrator and Haejoo" and "Minhyung." When Minhyung snubs Haejoo's taste in films on occasion, or comments on how he "envies" Haejoo, who's become "[a housewife who sits] around the house all day," Minhyung's misogyny is exposed, bringing the reader into the imagined empathetic network of "the narrator and Haejoo."

In this way, Haejoo's remark to the narrator—"I feel like it's gotten easier to talk with you about this stuff. Of course, it was easy before, too. But still."— alludes to another condition required for the alliance between them. If previously, their shared fury about Minhyung's misogyny was enough to unite Haejoo and the narrator, with these words, Haejoo explicitly indicates the fact that the narrator, who had been living as a gay man, has undergone gender affirmation surgery. That is to say, in this scene, the narrator and Haejoo recognize each other—or rather, Haejoo recognizes the narrator as "female" (a shorthand for having attained a physical congruence only

을 수 있는 상황에 부러 트랜스젠더 여성인 '나'를 놓아봄으로써 '나'의 "당황"을 해주 및 독자가 '관람'하도록 한다. 임신중절수술이 "그냥 혹 떼는 느낌"이었다는 해주의 말에 '나'는 "그래. 혹은 나도 떼봤는데, 별것 아니더라고."라고 애써 위로하지만, 이때 강조되는 것은 '나'와 해주의 '혹 떼기'가 결코 같을 수 없다는 점이다. 이 일련의 장면들은 해주가 '시스여성 고유의 경험'으로 간주되는 것을 트랜스여성인 '나'의 앞에서 과시적으로 전시하는 듯한 인상을 준다.

그런데 해주에게 부여된 이 혐의는 독자에 앞서 우선 '나'부터 오랫동안 의심해온 것이다. '나'가 해주를 위해 미역국을 끓이는 장면은 '나'가 태국에서 성전환수술 직후 "구아바 주스와 호박 수프" 같은 이국적인 음식을 먹으며 홀로 회복하던 장면과 병치되고, 드라이브 중 한 카페에 들어가 커피를 마시자는 해주의 제안은 "이태원 이외의 공간에서 치마를 입고 돌아다니는 일"이 아직 꺼려지는 '나'에게 꽤 둔감한 것으로 여겨진다. 무엇보다, '나'는 해주와 민형이 "딩크족 부부의 탄생" 축하파티에 하필 '나'를 부른 일, 해주가 임신중절수술 후 자신을 돌봐주었으면 했던 상대가 한동안 왕래가 없던 '나'였다는 점에는

through requisite medical means such as "surgery"), and thus they are able to "[snicker] like a pair of villains" together (calling to mind, the same way that a halo might appear above the head of a noble figure in a medieval work of art, the "gold outline" cast around Haejoo's head by the yellow light above the dining table).

But this alliance of "villains" is temporary. For instance, Haejoo—who has had an abortion—complains about her "breast pain," which "flusters" the narrator, who is unable to understand this. Seeing the narrator's confusion, Haejoo bursts out laughing. Thus, the story—by intentionally placing the narrator, a transgender woman, in a situation that only Haejoo, as a cisgender woman, can laugh at—allows the reader to observe the narrator's confusion alongside Haejoo. To Haejoo's comment that her abortion "feels like getting a lump removed," the narrator attempts to console her, replying, "Yeah. I got a lump removed, too, and it was no big deal," but the emphasis in this moment is placed on the fact that the narrator's "lump removal" and Haejoo's will never be the same. This series of scenes gives the impression that Haejoo is conspicuously displaying a "cis woman's unique experience" in front of a transgender woman.

But readers would have long had these suspicions

'나'가 "자녀를 둘 가능성이 전혀 없다는 것"이 계산됐으리라고 합리적으로 의심한다. '나'와 "나란히 앉아 마주보지 않아도 되"는 상황이 올 때까지 해주가 '나'의 근황을 묻지 않은 것은 배려일까, 무관심일까. 해주는 변해버린 민형/왕가위에게 배신감을 느끼지만, 해주와 '나' 역시 결코 서로에게 한결같은 존재는 아니다. 게다가 이어지는 에피소드는 해주와 '나'의 도덕적 위계를 따져보는 신중한 독자의 선택에 쐐기를 박는다. '나'가 해주-민형 부부와 멀어진 이유가 영화 〈가유희사〉에 나온 장국영의 여장에 대한 민형의 혐오, 그리고 당시 '나'가 "성전환" 수술비를 모으는 처지였다는 것. 이제 '나'가 겪은 소외와 "모욕"의 성격이 명백해진다.

여기까지 읽었을 때, 이 소설의 관심이 단지 (상상된) 동질성을 매개로 한 '우정'과 '여성연대'에만 있지 않음은 선연하다. 즉 소설은 독자의 동일시 대상을 '민형의 여성혐오를 매개로 형성된 '나-해주'의 여성연대'가 아니라, 시스젠더 헤테로 커플로부터 미묘한 차별과 타자화를 경험한 트랜스여성 '나'로 주의 깊게 이동시켰다. 이제 독자의 관심은 꽤 교묘하게 연출된 시스여성과 트랜스여성의 위계를 어떻게 봉합할 것인가에 있다.

of Haejoo, starting from the narrator. The scene where the narrator cooks seaweed soup for Haejoo is juxtaposed with the narrator's recollection of being all alone in Thailand immediately after her gender affirmation surgery, eating exotic food such as "guava juice and pumpkin soup," and Haejoo's suggestion during their drive that they stop inside a cafe for coffee could be viewed as quite inconsiderate of the narrator, who is "still somewhat reluctant to walk around in a skirt outside of Itaewon." Moreover, the narrator has reasonable suspicions that the reason why Haejoo and Minhyung call the narrator of all people over for the celebration of the "birth of a DINK couple," as well as why Haejoo chose the narrator, whom she hadn't seen for a while, as the person she wanted to take care of her following her abortion is because she had calculated that it "wasn't at all possible for the narrator to have kids." Is the fact that Haejoo doesn't ask the narrator at all about how she's been until they are in a situation where they are "sitting side by side, not having to look at each other" a form of consideration or disinterest? Haejoo feels a sense of betrayal because of the change in Minhyung/Wong Kar-wai, but of course, Haejoo and the narrator have never been constants for each other, either. In addition, the ep-

드라이브를 마친 '나'와 해주가 귀가했을 때, 민형이 등장한다. 해주가 민형과 대화를 나누는 동안 자리를 피해주는 '나'. 드디어 '나'에게 서장원 소설의 인장(印章)과도 같은 예의 그 '소요의 시간'이 주어진다. '나'는 "내가 치마를 입고 있다는 사실을 끝도 없이 상기시"키는 연분홍색 주름치마의 부스럭거리는 소리를 들으며 해주네 아파트 단지를 천천히 돌기 시작한다. 그리고 바로 이때, 해주와 독자 모두를 배반하는 '나'의 반란이 펼쳐진다.

늘 "해주의 불행을 반가워했다"는 '나'의 돌연한 고백. '나'는 해주가 임신을 포기하고, 민형과 이혼해 "홀로" 됨으로써 '나'와 "좀 더 많은 것을 공유할 수 있게 되기를 기대"했다고 되뇐다. "나의 유일한 친구"인 해주가 '나'처럼 "조금 더 마이너한 사람이 되어주길" 은밀히 바랐다는 것. 해주의 미래를 그렇게 상상한 뒤, 어디 있냐고 묻는 해주의 전화에 '나'는 "네게서 그리 멀지 않은 곳에 있다"고 답한다. 무슨 뜻일까.

일단, '나'의 대답의 함의를 짐작해 "네게서"라는 단어를 '여성에게서'라고 바꿔 적어보자. '여성'에게서 "그리 멀지 않은 곳"에 있는 '트랜스여성'. 그건 '트랜스여성은 여성'이라는 뜻으로도, 그 반대의 뜻으로도 읽힌다. 결국

isode that follows hammers home the fact that the reader has a careful choice to make in weighing the moral hierarchies of Haejoo and the narrator. The reason the narrator becomes estranged from the Haejoo-Minhyung couple is because of Minhyung's revulsion regarding Leslie Cheung's cross-dressing in the film *All's Well, Ends Well,* in addition to the narrator's situation, needing to save money to pay for her gender affirmation surgery. In this moment, the alienation the narrator has experienced and the nature of this "insult" become explicitly clear.

When you read up to this point, it is clear that the story's interest is not merely in the (imagined) oneness between "friendship" and "women's solidarity." In this story, rather than readers finding a target for their empathy in the narrator and Haejoo, an alliance formed as a result of Minhyung's misogyny, they are most deeply moved by the subtle discrimination and otherization the trans woman narrator has experienced from this cisgender, heterosexual couple. Now, the readers' interest lies in how the quite skillfully produced hierarchy of cis women and trans women might be redressed.

When the narrator and Haejoo return home from their drive, Minhyung is there. The narrator steps out while Haejoo and Minhyung converse. At last,

이 아포리아에 가까운 명제는 '나'와 해주가 어떻게 서로 "멀지 않은" 존재일 수 있는지 진지하게 생각해보자는 제언이다. 여성혐오의 피해자로서? 여성성기의 해부학적 동일성으로서? 재생산에 무능하거나 혹은 재생산권이 박탈된 존재로서? '소수자'의 위상을 나눠 가진 '비주류'로서?

하지만 누구에게도 환영받지 못할 '나'의 이 갑작스런 고백은 뭘 위한 것일까. 어쩌면 서사 내내 수동적인 태도로 일관해온 '나'의 도발적인 내면은 그간 트랜스젠더/소수자를 '불쌍한 피해자'로만 묘사해온 한국문학사의 오랜 관성을 거스르기 위한 것일 수도 있다. 다만, 그 독해는 석연치 않다. 갑자기 누설된 '나'의 은밀한 욕망은 해주와 '나'의 관계를 "'마이너'한 존재들의 우정"이라고 아름답게 읽고 싶은 독자들에게는 너무나 버석거리기 때문이다.

그렇다면 이 결말은 누구에게 안도감을 줄까. 게이/트랜스젠더 친구의 우정을 착취해온 해주, 이 이야기를 '여성연대'를 도모하는 매끄러운 서사로 읽고 싶은 이들에게 이 결말은 어떻게 읽힐까. 소설의 중반부가 해주의 필요에 따라 선별적으로 소환돼온 '나'의 경험을 서술함으

Seo's story affords the narrator some of that "meandering time" that has become his signature. Listening to the rustle and swish of her light pink pleated skirt, which "[makes her] acutely aware of the fact that [she is] wearing it," the narrator slowly begins to circle Haejoo's apartment complex. And at that exact moment, the narrator's revolt against Haejoo and the reader alike is set into motion.

The narrator's abrupt confession that she has always "delighted in Haejoo's misfortune." The hope she voices that Haejoo's "aloneness" after giving up on her pregnancy and divorcing Minhyung "would be yet another thing [they] shared." The secret desire the narrator has that Haejoo, "the only friend [she] had," will be pushed "further and further into the margins." After imagining this sort of future for Haejoo, the narrator answers a phone call from Haejoo asking where she is with the reply: "not too far from where you are." What could this mean?

First of all, let's assume that the narrator's reply "from where you are" can be changed to "from where women are"—the transgender narrator's position in relation to "where women are." This can be read as meaning that "trans women are women," and also with the opposite meaning. In the end, this proposition—which is almost an irresolvable con-

로써 바로 그 독자들의 죄책감을 환기했다면, 해주의 불행을 소망해왔다는 '나'의 내면을 의도적으로 노출시킨 후반부는 다시 그 독자들의 피상적인 정의감에 꽤 효과적인 알리바이를 제공하는 것 같다. 그러니 확인해볼 일이다. 혹시 "네게서 그리 멀지 않은 곳에 있다"는 말이 우정이라기보다는 '도전'이나 '위협'처럼 들리지는 않았는가. 반전의 장치로서 사용된 트랜스젠더의 퍼스널리티는 누구에게 심리적 편안함을 선사하는가. 해주의 머리 위에 또 한 번 "금빛 테두리"를 만들지는 않는가?

더 과감하고 매혹적인 상상도 가능하다. 한국문화사에서 여성 간의 친밀성에 대한 욕구가 종종 '동일성'에의 욕구로 (부정확하게) 재현돼온 관성을 상기하자면, '나'와 해주의 성별은 물론, '비혼·무자녀'라는 조건마저 동일해지기를 바라는 '나'의 욕망, 비록 연락을 먼저 끊은 것은 '나'지만, 해주의 연락을 은근히 기다려온 '나'의 감정의 드라마는 해주에 대해 억압해온 '나'의 독점적 친밀성에의 욕망을 암시할 수도 있다. 특히 해주와 민형의 커플링이 '나'의 도움으로 가능했고, 민형 아닌 '나'가 해주의 연인으로 오해받곤 했다는 진술을 고려할 때, "네게서 그리 멀지 않은 곳에 있다"는 '나'의 대답은 한 트랜스젠더 레

tradiction—suggests that we should think earnestly about whether the narrator and Haejoo can, in fact, exist "not too far from" each other. As victims of misogyny? Alike in that they are anatomically female? Or else in that they are unable to reproduce or have been deprived of their reproductive rights? That they belong to a "marginalized group" and have their statuses as "minorities" in common?

But what is to be made of the narrator's sudden confession that no one could possibly accept? It might be that this provocative inner side of the narrator, which is perhaps consistent with the passive attitude that the narrator has shown throughout the story, is meant to go against the longstanding law of inertia in Korean literature by which transgender people/minorities are rendered only as "pitiful victims." Still, that reading is uncertain. This secret wish of ill will that the narrator suddenly divulges will greatly rattle readers who want to read beauty into Haejoo and the narrator's relationship, a "friendship between those living marginal existences."

In that case, would this ending grant some readers a sense of relief? How might this ending and Haejoo, who has exploited her friendship with her gay/transgender friend, be read by those who want to see the story as a smooth narrative that aims to pro-

즈비언(혹은 트랜스젠더 바이섹슈얼, 혹은 다른 무엇)의 대담하고도 불온한 욕망에 대한 강렬한 예고처럼 들린다.

아무튼 소설은 여기서 멈췄다. 그건 이 지점이야말로 독자가 자신의 윤리와 쾌락법칙을 스스로 투영하고 발명해야 하는 결정적 장소라는 뜻이다. "네게서 그리 멀지 않은 곳"에 있는데도, 우리는 타인의 욕망에 대해 그토록 무지하기에.

mote "women's solidarity"? If the middle of the story evokes a sense of guilt in those readers through the descriptions of the narrator's experience being selected and summoned according to Haejoo's needs, the latter half of the story in which the narrator intentionally discloses the inner self that wishes for Haejoo's misfortune seems to provide a rather effective alibi for those same readers' shallow sense of justice. Thus, this is something to look further into. Perhaps rather than indicating a friendship, might the words "not too far from where you are" be understood as a "challenge" or a "threat"? To whom might the personality of a transgender person, used as a tool of reversal, offer psychological comfort? Does this not create yet another "gold outline" around Haejoo's head?

A bolder and more captivating vision is possible. If we recall that, throughout the cultural history of Korea, women's desires for intimacy have on occasion been (inaccurately) reimagined as desires for "oneness," the narrator's desire to become "like" Haejoo in terms of gender, of course, and even in terms of being "unmarried, without children," as well as the emotional drama of the narrator secretly awaiting Haejoo's call, could suggest a suppressed desire for exclusive intimacy, even though the narrator was the one who first cut off contact with Haejoo. In particular, when we consider the fact that Haejoo and Minhyung's coupling was made possible with the narrator's help, and that it was the narrator, not Minhyung, who was mistaken as Haejoo's lover, the narrator's reply of "not too far from where you are" sounds like an urgent forewarning of one transgender lesbian's (or transgender bisexual's, etc.) bold and rebellious desire.

In any case, the story ends here. Meaning this is precisely the designated place for the reader to project and devise their own ethics and principles of pleasure. Ignorant, to an extent—even as we are "not too far from where you are"—about the desires of others.

비평의 목소리
Critical Acclaim

서장원의 「해피 투게더」는 이제 다시는 되돌아갈 수 없는 지나간 시간에 관한 소설이라고 할 수 있다. 누군가는 과거의 자신으로는 더 이상 살고 싶지 않은 것이다. 어쩌면 「해피 투게더」는 절대로 넘을 수 없는 어떤 선에 관한 소설이기도 하다. 이 작품에서는 해주의 남편이자 화자인 '나'의 친구인 '민형'이 가장 선명한 선을 가졌다. 그는 장국영이 B급 영화에 출연해 별 볼일 없는 연기를 하는 게 참을 수 없다. 어쩌면 그건 민형의 세계관이다. 또 왕가위는 좋아해도 로만 폴란스키를 지지할 수 없는 건 민형의 아내인 '해주'의 세계관이다. 모두들 각자 넘을 수 있거나 넘을 수 없는, 각자의 바운더리 안에서, 친하거나

Seo Jang-won's *Happy Together* could be said to be a story about days past, a time to which we can never return. A story about someone no longer wanting to live as their past self. At the same time, *Happy Together* may also be about certain lines that can never be crossed. In the story, Minhyung—Haejoo's husband and the narrator's friend—maintains the clearest of these lines. He can't stand Leslie Cheung's mediocre acting in B-movies. This is perhaps reflective of his outlook on the world. Meanwhile, as much as his wife Haejoo loves Wong Kar-wai, she cannot support Roman Polanski. All of them, each within their own traversable or untraversable boundaries, either grow closer or start to argue, band together

싸우거나 연대하거나 혐오한다. 트랜스젠더인 내가 해주를, 임신을 중지하고 이혼하는 해주가 나를 보살필 수 있게 된 건 바로 그 선 때문이다. 그리고 나와 해주는 이제 과거의 삶과는 결별한다.

왕가위의 〈해피 투게더〉가 제작되고 2년 후 발표된 메이킹 필름 〈부에노스 아이레스 제로 디그리〉(1999)에서 왕가위는 말한다. "동쪽도 서쪽도 아닌, 밤도 낮도 아닌, 춥지도 덥지도 않은 어떤 곳을 상상했고 부에노스 아이레스로 갔다."라고. 서장원도 왕가위처럼 현실에는 없는 영토를 상상한다. 최소한 거기에서는 넘지 못할 선이란 없고, 모두들 평화롭게 서로를 지켜볼 수 있다.

강영숙(소설가)

서장원의 「해피 투게더」는 표면에서 발견되는 관계의 변수와 이면에 존재하는 관계의 상수가 만들어내는 관계의 법칙을 형상화 한 작품이다. 젊은이들이 10여년에 걸쳐 경험하는 복잡다단한 관계의 변화를 통해 이 작품은 타자와 함께 살아간다는 것의 어려움과 비정함을 담담하게 전달하고 있다. 무엇보다도 타인의 불행이나 결핍을 통해서만 유지되는 관계의 섬찟한 상수를 확인하는 것이

or grow to loathe each other. It is precisely because of these boundaries that Haejoo is able to ask the transgender narrator to care for her as she terminates her pregnancy and goes through a divorce. After, the narrator and Haejoo also become divorced from their past lives.

In *Buenos Aires Zero Degree* (1999), the behind-the-scenes documentary for *Happy Together* released two years after the film, Wong Kar-wai says: "I imagined a place that was neither East nor West, night nor day, cold nor hot, and I went to Buenos Aires." Like Wong Kar-wai, Seo Jang-won imagines a realm that does not exist in reality. In that realm, at least, there are no lines that cannot be crossed, and everyone there can observe one another in peace.

Kang Young-sook(Writer)

Seo Jang-won's *Happy Together* is a work shaped by the law of relationships, which in turn is shaped by both the surface-level variables and underlying constants of connection. In exploring the complex changes in relationships these young people experience over the course of a decade, the story even-handedly conveys the downfalls and difficulties of living with others. Moreover, the simultaneous pain and beauty of reading this story is seeing confirma-

이 소설을 읽는 고통이자 묘미라고 할 수 있다. 인간은 타인과 자신의 불행을 재는 너무도 섬세한 내면의 저울을 지니고 있으며, 이 저울이 균형을 이루었을 때만 비로소 인간은 상대방을 향해 손을 내밀 수 있다는 것이 관계의 한 가지 법칙인 것이다. 그러한 관계의 엄연한 진실은 주인공 '나'와 해주가 시공을 뛰어넘어서 느꼈던 가슴통증을 통해 감각적으로 표현되어 있다. 이 가슴통증이 별나지 않은 방식으로, 은은하지만 진중한 방식으로 드러나 있다는 점에서 이 작가의 미래에 기대를 걸어본다.

이경재(문학평론가)

「해피 투게더」는 매력적인 마지막 문장을 가진 소설이다.

"나는 그저 네게서 그리 멀지 않은 곳에 있다고만 대답했다." 이 문장이 이 소설의 지도가 아닐까 싶다. 소설이 거느린 키워드들은 코로나 시절, 트랜스젠더, 임신중단, 이혼, 돌봄, 영화동아리, 우정과 같은, 낯익은 소재들이다. 낯익은 풍경들로 흘러가던 소설은 "나는 언제나 해주의 불행을 반가워했다"라는, 거의 막바지에 이른 문장부터 반전 같은 차이를 만들어내고 있다. 소수자에 대한

tion of the horrifying constant that is a relationship maintained only through the misfortunes or short-comings of others. It is one of the principles of relationships that humans weigh their own misfortunes and those of others on a delicate internal scale, and only when this scale is balanced can people reach out and offer each other a hand. This undeniable truth of such relationships is viscerally conveyed through the chest pains Haejoo and the narrator experience across different times and spaces. That this chest pain is revealed not in an unusual way, but in a subtle, serious manner, leads me to eagerly anticipate the future of this writer.

Lee Kyung-jae(Literary Critic)

Happy Together is a story that ends with a stunning last line. "... [All] I said was, I'm close by, not too far from where you are." I wonder whether this sentence isn't a map of the entire story. Its keywords— the COVID era, transgender identity, abortion, divorce, caretaking, film clubs, friendship—are familiar subject matter. The story moves through familiar landscapes, then crafts a reversal starting from one of the near-final lines: "I had always delighted in Haejoo's misfortune." The strength of the story is in the tension that arises when one reads

'덤덤한 인정 태도' 정도로 이 소설의 장점을 읽어내려 가던 독법에 긴장이 생긴다. 친구가 좀 더 마이너한 사람이 되어주길 간절히 바라는 이 사나운 마음은 복잡한 감정을 불러일으킨다. 트랜스젠더 레즈비언이라는 이중의 성 정체성. 마이너리티 중의 마이너리티. 물론 나는 서장원 작가가 특이한 소재에 주목했다고 생각지 않는다. 우정이든 사랑이든 불가해한 감정에 내재한 복잡성을 마지막 몇 문장은 보여준다. 사랑의 폭력성에 대한 이야기도 아니다. 사랑이, 우정이 그렇게 복잡하다는 태도로 봐야 할 것이다. 그래서 "나는 그저 네게서 그리 멀지 않은 곳에 있다"라는 따뜻하기도 하고 서늘하기도 한 문장이 단단해 보인다.

전성태(소설가)

서장원의 「해피 투게더」는 '퀴어'라는 성소수자 문제를 다루고 있으나, 퀴어문학이라 소개하고 싶지 않다. '퀴어'에 대한 문제의식보다는 인물들 사이에 배음처럼 흐르는 감정의 전면화가 더 인상적이기 때문이다. 그것은 어쩌면 서장원 작가의 특장일지도 모른다. 날카롭게 벼려진 칼날 대신, 그 칼날에 스치는 구름과 바람소리 같은 것을

with an attitude of mere "placid acknowledgement" of minorities. This fierce, sincere desire to see a friend further relegated to the margins evokes some complicated emotions. The dual gender identity of a transgender lesbian. A minority among minorities. Of course, I do not believe Seo Jang-won focuses on this subject matter because it is unusual. The last several sentences show us the inherent complexity of these inscrutable emotions, whether friendship or love. This is not a story about the violence of love. Rather, it is an invitation to view love and friendship in a complex way. "I'm close by, not too far from where you are." That single line, at turns both warm and cool, seems to be firm to the touch.

Jeon Sung-tae(Writer)

Seo Jang-won's *Happy Together* deals with "queer" issues, but I don't want to introduce the work as one of queer literature. This is because, rather than a conscious awareness of "queerness," the much more impressive aspect of the story is the harmonious, full-scale flow of emotions from one character to another. This is perhaps Seo Jang-won's signature. The way he captures, not the sharpened blade of a knife, but the sound of the wind and clouds grazing the blade. Paradoxically, the blade resounds more

담아내는 것. 역설적으로 이 서정적 풍경을 통해 칼날은 더 크게 울리고 더 강렬하게 빛난다.

「해피투게더」에서 대학동기 세 명의 관계는, 동성애와 이성애로 갈리면서 안전해지고, 다시 우정과 사랑으로 갈리면서 위태로워진다. 그러나 작가는 이 갈림들 사이에 트랜스젠더인 '나'의 미로 같은 감정선을 숨겨놓는다. '해주'로부터 늘 그리 멀지 않은 곳에 존재하는 '나'가 지닌 진짜 사랑의 정체성은 무엇인가? 이 소설이 끝나는 즈음에 이 물음을 놓고 있는 작가의 교묘한 솜씨가 놀랍다.

정은경(문학평론가)

loudly and gleams more brightly through this lyrical landscape.

The three college classmates' relationship in *Happy Together* is made secure by the divisions between homosexuality and heterosexuality, and it is made precarious again by the divide between friendship and love. Yet the writer conceals the transgender narrator's labyrinth of emotions within these divisions. Just what is the true nature of the narrator's love, this narrator who always exists not too far from where Haejoo is? At the end of this story, readers are left in awe at the subtle hand of the writer who poses this question.

Jung Eun-kyoung(Literary Critic)

K-픽션 029
해피 투게더

2021년 4월 20일 초판 1쇄 발행

지은이 서장원 | **옮긴이** 페이지 모리스 | **펴낸이** 김재범
기획위원 전성태, 정은경, 이경재, 강영숙
인쇄·제책 굿에그커뮤니케이션 | **종이** 한솔PNS
펴낸곳 (주)아시아 | **출판등록** 2006년 1월 27일 제406-2006-000004호
주소 경기도 파주시 회동길 445
전화 031.955.7958 | **팩스** 031.955.7956 | **홈페이지** www.bookasia.org
ISBN 979-11-5662-173-7(세트) | 979-11-5662-533-9 (04810)
값은 뒤표지에 있습니다.

K-Fiction 029
Happy Together

Written by Seo Jang-won | Translated by Paige Aniyah Morris
Published by ASIA Publishers | 445, Hoedong-gil, Paju-si, Gyeonggi-do, Korea
Homepage Address www.bookasia.org | Tel.(8231).955.7958 | Fax.(8231).955.7956
First published in Korea by ASIA Publishers 2021
ISBN 979-11-5662-173-7(set) | 979-11-5662-533-9 (04810)

바이링궐 에디션 한국 대표 소설 set 3

K-픽션 한국 젊은 소설

최근에 발표된 단편소설 중 가장 우수하고 흥미로운 작품을 엄선하여 출간하는 〈K-픽션〉은 한국문학의 생생한 현장을 국내외 독자들과 실시간으로 공유하고자 기획되었습니다. 원작의 재미와 품격을 최대한 살린 〈K-픽션〉 시리즈는 매 계절마다 새로운 작품을 선보입니다.

K-포엣 시리즈는 계속됩니다.
리스트에 변동이 있을 수 있습니다.